Albert Goes Hollywood

story *by* HENRY SCHWARTZ

pictures *by* AMY SCHWARTZ

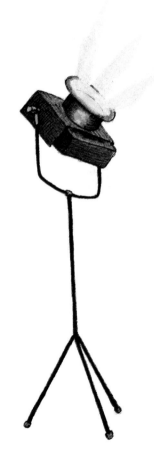

ORCHARD BOOKS   NEW YORK

For Joan, Debbie, and Becky
—H.S. and A.S.

Orchard Books, 387 Park Avenue South, New York, NY 10016

Manufactured in the United States of America. Printed by General Offset Company, Inc. Bound by
Horowitz/Rae. Book design by Mina Greenstein. The text of this book is set in 16 point Schneidler. The
illustrations are pen-and-ink with watercolor wash, reproduced in full color.
10 9 8 7 6 5 4 3 2 1

Library of Congress Cataloging-in-Publication Data
Schwartz, Henry. Albert goes Hollywood / story by Henry Schwartz ; pictures by Amy Schwartz.
p.   cm. "A Richard Jackson book." Summary: Liz gets to keep her pet dinosaur Albert when
she finds him a job in the movies.   ISBN 0-531-05980-4.   ISBN 0-531-08580-5 (lib. bdg.)
[1. Dinosaurs—Fiction. 2. Motion pictures—Fiction.] I. Schwartz, Amy, ill.
II. Title. PZ7.S4077A1 1992 [E]—dc20 91-18495

Albert is my pet. I captured him on a camping trip in Baja California.

Mom and Dad and I brought him home to Los Angeles to live with us.

Albert is a big help around the house. He trims the palm tree on the front lawn and cleans our second story window with Dad.

And once he scared off a burglar.

Everybody loves Albert. The PTA even agreed to pay his food bill if I would take him around to schools.

Sometimes I take Albert to my own, Surfside Elementary. He sits in back of the classroom because he's so shy. But at recess he's a whiz on a skateboard. And he plays goalie on my soccer team, the Dino-Mites. Nobody scores a goal on Albert.

The only problem with Albert is that he eats like a horse. Mom feeds him 100 pounds of chicken wings a day, if they're on sale at the market. Usually she makes him 250 hamburgers, with all the fixings. I told Mom to hold the relish because Albert doesn't like pickles.

It was a terrible day at school when my teacher, Mrs. Fegelman, told me the PTA couldn't pay Albert's food bill any longer.

At dinner Dad said, "Liz, Albert is going to eat us out of house and home. I'm afraid we've got to give him to the zoo."

I ran crying to Albert in the backyard. He lowered his neck to me, and I flung my arms around him. I told him I would never, ever give him up. He grunted. I sort of think he understood.

I decided then and there to get Albert a new job. I went inside to my desk and made up business cards.

Have your picture taken with Albert!

DINOSAUR SERVICE
222-2222

DINO RIDES   KITE RESCUE

I gave out the cards around town. Albert got only one call. He was hired to carry sandwich boards up and down Wilshire Boulevard. But the pavement was too hard on his feet.

Then he worked as a lifeguard at Santa Monica beach. Albert rescued a whole family from drowning. But it was only a summer job.

Dad said we had to take Albert to the zoo to show him his new home. I knew he would hate it. He did. I had to think of something.

On the way home I had an idea. I talked Dad into stopping for a soda. I asked him to pull in at this famous drugstore in Hollywood. My best friend in school had told me that lots of movie stars have been discovered there. I thought maybe Albert could break into the movies and make zillions of dollars.

We sat at the counter, sipping our sodas. Dad and I had chocolate. Albert had butterscotch. I heard a small man in a booth talking to another.

"What we need is a big new movie star," he said. "You know, like King Kong. The strong, silent type."

I coughed loudly. The small man looked up, and I pointed to Albert.

"CO-LOSS-AL!" he screamed.

He told us he was a director over at MOGO Studios. And he asked us to bring Albert in that very afternoon for a screen test!

At the studio Albert and I were taken to makeup.
Next we were led into a very large room. There were other animals standing around, waiting for their screen tests.
The director pointed to a kangaroo. Then he stepped behind the camera and shouted, "Lights! Camera! Action!"
The kangaroo hopped onto the set. A little kangaroo stood up in her pouch. Someone put on a cassette of "I Get a Kick Out of You," and the mother and baby began jumping about.
"No competition," I whispered to Albert.

Next came a hippo in ballet shoes.
"Out! Out!" yelled the director.

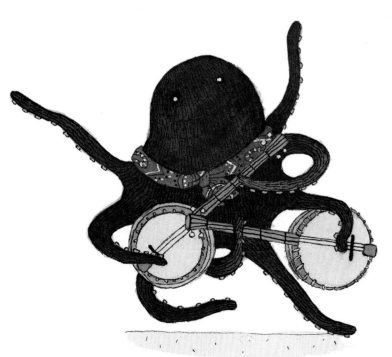

Then an octopus sidled onstage
playing "Dueling Banjos."
"Er, unusual," said the director.

At last it was Albert's turn.

"Lights! Camera! Action!"

Albert just stood there. Frozen.

"Cut! Cut!" shouted the director. "Let's call it a day."

I jumped out of my chair. "Please, Mr. Director, Albert's just camera shy. Won't you give him another chance?"

"Oh, all right," he said. "Lights! Camera! Action!"

I had an idea. I slid my skateboard over to Albert. His eyes lit up. He jumped on the board and did fancy figure eights. Then he executed a perfect loop-de-loop.

"STU-PEN-DOUS!" screamed the director, jumping up and down and waving his arms. "Albert wins! Now we can make a movie!"

"I have a neat idea for a movie," I said. I told him how I had captured Albert in Mexico with hamburgers.

"OUT-RA-GEOUS!" the director yelled. "It's a wrap!"

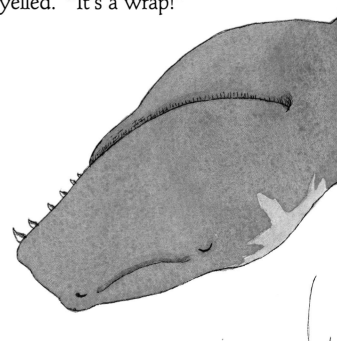

MOGO Studios took us down to Baja on location. Albert and I got to play ourselves. Famous movie stars played Mom and Dad.

I had my own dressing room in a trailer. For Albert, they put two trailers together. Each door had a star.

I was Albert's coach. The director told me what he
wanted him to do. Then I showed him.
And Albert did all his own stunts.

We recreated my first meeting with Albert, and how Mom
got so scared. I showed the actress who played Mom how to
climb up and off the van. And I helped Albert remember
what it had been like to eat his first hot dog.

Between takes Albert brought me to some of his favorite childhood spots.

When we finished shooting, the studio took us around Los Angeles to get publicity shots. Albert loved the La Brea tar pits.

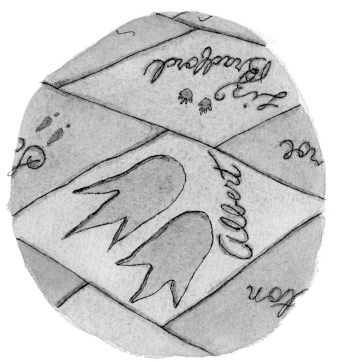

We were invited to Mann's Chinese Theater in Hollywood. I put my hand prints in fresh cement. Albert put in his footprints.

Soon it was the night of the premiere. I was very nervous.
Our whole future hung on this movie. The studio sent a
stretch limo to our house. We all climbed in.

As we got near the theater, I saw searchlights playing against the sky. Fans were sitting in bleachers on the sidewalk. Mrs. Fegelman and my entire third grade class were there! Everybody clapped when we got out.

But how would the people inside like the movie?

We found our seats, the lights dimmed, and the picture began. There I was on-screen, setting out hamburgers for Albert. I wished I'd worn my red barrette. Then Albert appeared. The audience went wild! They whistled and cheered! They loved him!

When the movie ended, Albert got a standing ovation.
The director ran up to us, waving a contract.
"ALBERT, BABY! You've got it made!"
And we had. Albert had a job, and I had Albert.